Last Hope

A short story by
Douglas Van Dyke Jr.

Originally published in
"Otherworldly: A Genre Fiction
Anthology, Vol 1"

Last Hope

Douglas Van Dyke Jr., author, publishing this edition under company name Dhea Loral. "Last Hope" by Douglas Van Dyke Jr. was originally published, and remains in print, in "Otherworldly: A Genre Fiction Anthology, Volume 1" hosted by Nerd Street in 2024. It is printed here with full printing, publishing, and distribution rights of "Otherworldly: A Genre Fiction Anthology, Volume 1" publisher, Lucy's Lantern Literature.

ISBN: 978-1-949060-16-4

Written by Douglas Van Dyke Jr
Please Visit: http://dhealoral.com

Table of Contents

Author's Introduction

Dear Reader,

This is a short story, originally offered and still in print in "Otherworldly: A Genre Fiction Anthology, Volume 1" hosted by Nerd Street, published by Lucy's Lantern Literature. I am offering it to you at a low price, (some may have acquired this for free), for your entertainment.

I hope you like this sample enough to check out my website, books, and social media listed at the end. I've written a few novels praised with good reviews, won some awards, and I have too many stories in my head to slow down my writing any time soon. Most of my novels are different series in the same fantasy world, in which characters and events can cross over series. However, I've also branched out into other genres through numerous anthology submissions. Please see my website at DheaLoral.com for a complete up-to-date list of my work.

In the end of this manuscript, you will see more ways to connect with me.

Sincerely, Douglas Van Dyke Jr

Last Hope

Gordon Rogers moved with a purpose through a maze of neon-lit, smoke-fogged alleys, believing he was in the perfect environment to find his prey. They called this multi-level mess of concrete backstreets the Toy Maze, and many considered it the most disreputable part of town. A young, rebellious crowd devised all sorts of ways to use their mutations irresponsibly in the cover of its evening shadows and private alleys. Gordon, a fit man in his mid-thirties, couldn't fault them for using their abilities to find some pleasurable release. The whole planet was going to hell, although most didn't realize the depth of the problem. He saw Lightweavers producing humanoid illusions, which danced to the tune that Soundmixers created out of nonexistent instruments, while groupies inhaled colorful clouds of some funny gas that a Windmixer had added to the air. One man, an Elastic, had one of his arms looped three times around a young lady's arm. She didn't seem to mind, since she was laughing at some comment he made. Some of the chronicled mutations allowed their host to undergo physical alterations, such as the middle-aged man handing out drinks with tentacle-arms. Other mutations allowed mental hallucinations, and there seemed to be no shortage of young people who would pay for a temporary mind trip. Some rebels sheltered under the pyramid lights of the streetlamps, others clung to disreputable companions in the shadows. Gordon considered most of their hobbies harmless, at least to anyone other than themselves.

Decades of government gene-seeding and mutations resulted in all modern-day humans having at least one special ability. Though they had unlocked some incredible potential, the genetic manipulation had its shortcomings. Scientists had no control over what ability would manifest in an individual. One side-effect included mutations creating some real monsters. Tonight, one stalked the Toy Maze.

As Gordon navigated the alleys, his eyes took the time to focus on every person he passed. He methodically searched for his quarry, looking for hints of a specific talent. He entered the influence of other people's abilities as he moved. Their powers allowed them to create illusions, conjurations, magnetism, acoustics, and other extensions of power in the air. Gordon felt their abilities like waves of energy pulsing against his skin, making it tingle. As he hunted, he tried to quell his own ability from responding. If he allowed his mutation to be fully released, it would unmask him and generate unwanted attention. His hunt was hindered by alleyways saturated with strong vibes of power, forcing him to navigate detours.

One discreet side-passage revealed the symptoms he sought. Three individuals lie sprawled on the concrete, holding tightly to their guts. They moaned in discomfort. As best as Gordon could tell, none of them radiated any aura of their powers. The hunter couldn't determine anyone's specific power in the absence of obvious manifestations which could be seen or heard. He only knew that this group wasn't reaching out with their abilities, since his skin couldn't feel those eddies of power fluctuating through the air. The lack of use helped to confirm that these three were not faking their sickness.

"Did you all get sick at once?" Gordon Rogers inquired.

"Must have been that foreign buffet place. Dammit, Kyle." One groaned.

The other coughed his response. "Go lose yourself, man. I thought you could neutralize any impurities."

The young men could have gotten some bad food, as they had assumed, but the hunter suspected it was something out of their hands.

Gordon said, "Listen to me, I don't like repeating myself. Did you all fall sick at once? As in, within a few seconds of each other?"

One waved a feeble attempt to shoo their intruder. "Yeah man, that stuff hit us suddenly, then we dropped like dominoes. So what?"

But he already left them, knowing that he followed the right trail. He'd studied people and predicted their patterns. Small groups of people were getting sick, most of them had probably been too oblivious of their surroundings from the start. Gordon's instinct told him that the one responsible wouldn't be foolish enough to try that in too large a crowd. He'd already set off certain government monitors, though the culprit likely didn't realize he had set off alarms.

Gordon Rogers spotted something suspicious rounding a corner. He saw a young man: barely past his teens, typical punk look, spiky hairstyle in a blend of red and orange colors, wearing a ripped-sleeve, neon-striped jacket. By itself, his appearance didn't make him stand out compared to many others Gordon witnessed that night. Instead, it was the manner in which the young man skulked around a corner, resembling another hunter tailing some prey. It helped that he had already studied a photo of his quarry. Gordon recognized enough of the man's features to know that this was Zollo – not his real name, just an alias he'd chosen on the Netboard.

Even as he watched, Gordon remained far enough away so as to not raise any undue suspicion. A couple, eyes only for each other, stood a casual distance away. If Zollo looked in his direction, Gordon might seem more like the uncomfortable third bicycle wheel alongside the two lovers, rather than another hunter.

Zollo did scan his surroundings, his suspicious eyes scanned right past Gordon as the middle-aged man pretended to be punching a text into his mobile. Feeling confident that no one seemed to be paying attention, Zollo returned his attention to peeping around a corner. He raised his hand, revealing to his skulker that he might be ready to unleash a mutant ability.

Gordon felt the urge to interfere, but resisted. He needed to be absolutely certain of both Zollo's intentions and ability. Besides, if this truly was the guilty party he'd been seeking, then the damage Zollo inflicted could be cured easily. Gordon couldn't feel the ripple of the punk's ability from this distance, but he knew something seemed to issue forth. Zollo finished whatever effect he desired, expressed an unfriendly smile, then moved further down the dark street. As soon as the punk was out of sight, Gordon pocketed his phone and hurried to the corner.

The scene before him mimicked the earlier encounter. Two young people were doubled over in the alley, one of them retching her guts out. He no longer held any doubt that this was Zollo, and that this young man's mutant ability had carried out previous assaults reported in the city. Government sensors had become adept at tracking the use of genetic powers, but couldn't always pinpoint the user associated with them. It didn't help that some people tried to misrepresent their powers, despite a mandate for everyone to test and register their ability by age fourteen. Some scaled back on their power or found a way to mimic a different effect in order to be registered with a lackluster ability. Many had plenty of reasons for wanting the government to overlook their potential.

Now that Gordon had properly identified his quarry, the chase commenced. He quick-stepped in the direction he'd seen the punk depart. Despite his attempt at stealth, he turned a corner just as Zollo happened to be watching for anyone trailing him. They locked stares. Zollo's eyes grew wide as he guessed the intent of his pursuer.

This time, the younger man eschewed subtlety and raised his arms to attack. Gordon no longer tried to suppress his own power. The older hunter kept advancing on Zollo despite the ripple of energy waves tingling against his skin. The spiky-haired punk must have been trying to make his stalker nauseous, but his ability didn't harm Gordon at all. The only sensation felt was a tingling of the older man's skin. Zollo grunted as he tried to pour all of his power into the attack. The young man's curled fingers began to tremble. All of his efforts had no effect. Nullifiers such as Gordon were the antithesis of all other mutated powers. His ability counteracted any other talent aimed at him.

Gordon shouted, "Cease right now!"

He planned to say more, but Zollo turned and ran. Gordon sprinted after him in pursuit. This time, he didn't try to hold his power in check. It took mental effort to restrain himself, and the act could leave him vulnerable to Zollo's power. The ensuing pursuit banished all subtlety. One hunter chased another, leaving innocent civilians stepping out of the way.

The Toy Maze wound around itself, earning its namesake. Multiple-level walkways, stairways, ladders, and dead-ends led between a number of doors but few windows. Those who owned parts of the property and wielded influence here loved it the way it existed

Zollo led Gordon Rogers on a chase which constantly veered direction and managed to blow through small groups of people. Party-goers cursed and waved rude gestures when Zollo barreled past them. A true panic set in when Gordon followed, his ability undoing the powers of everyone he passed. Illusions of light and sound dispersed in his presence. The chase raced past the elastic man whose arm still encircled a girl's. Gordon's power nullified the ability, resulting in both parties screaming as the arm painfully whipped back into a more natural state.

Zollo vaulted a railing into a lower courtyard. He gasped in a quick breath as he looked back. Gordon performed the same trick and gained on him. Behind both, a crowd of people were left screaming and crying for answers.

The young man only succeeded in outrunning his endurance. Zollo had never run so hard in his life. Usually, his power was enough to make sure no one ever gave him trouble.

On the other hand, Gordon's power offered him no special bonus in life. His ability only temporarily nullified anyone with whom he came into contact. That brought engagements down to a physical matchup; usually against humans who relied on a bolstered physique from their powers. Gordon kept himself in peak athletic shape for just this reason. He'd also trained in parkour-style runs. As a result, rebellious punks like Zollo never stood a realistic chance at outrunning him.

Other witnesses watched in shock as Gordon tackled Zollo in the middle of a small courtyard. The two runners flipped over a park bench as they crashed to a stop. Both the questionable action and the loud snap of a bench board pulled everyone's attention to them.

For all Zollo's struggles, he began to hyperventilate when Gordon managed to CLINK one of his arms into the handcuffs. He said, "What do you expect, man? The only power life gave me was to make other people sick. I didn't kill anyone, or even hurt them that badly. Surely there are worse vices to pursue out there." His plea had no effect, so he turned to a threat. "If you take me in, I'll make everyone here so sick, they'll be comatose in a hospital."

"No, you won't." Gordon replied with hardly a sweat. "These cuffs are coated in a gene substance resembling my Nullifier ability. You won't be able to use your power now."

Accentuating his statement, he snapped the second one in place. His victim began to howl obscenities.

The older man sighed. "As for your antics, you can't assault dozens of people each month and expect that to go unpunished. Not to mention, I'm guessing you faked your true ability on official documents."

At this point, Gordon reached for his phone to call in a pickup squad. He noticed all the eyes staring at him in curiosity. Some of them looked aggressive, eyeing him like he was intruding on their turf.

He announced, "Federal investigator, RE operative. I need everyone to stand back…"

Everyone knew that RE meant “Rogue Enforcement.” This was a man that the government sent in to deal with people whose powers had become a problem.

Panic set in for most everyone else. The rest of them scattered throughout the Toy Maze to find a place to hide. That’s how the populace acted when they realized they had a real monster in their midst.

***

Trevor Snyder sat on the couch, spending his youth engrossed in the television. His butt relaxed into the same custom impression formed by habit over the course of his life. It's not that he didn't favor the outdoors. In truth, the teenager would have liked nothing better than to have an adventure in the woods, try to learn fishing, or even walk the miles necessary to get to the closest ice cream place.

The home in which he and his father lived would have been perfect for such pursuits. They enjoyed a mountain view, as remote as anyone could have wanted. The only reason Trevor even knew they had neighbors came from the sight of chimney smoke at other spots in the mountains. They never visited anyone, nor did anyone ever check up on them. He could likely pick a random direction, walk for a few hours, and still not see another person.

He couldn't remember seeing more than a handful of people over the course of his life.

He and his father never traveled. Trevor rarely came within eyesight of the closest small village. They didn't own a phone, owned the same car for as long as he could remember, and his father worried endlessly that the boy would somehow injure himself and require a hospital visit.

“We’re living off the grid.” His father, Dylan, would often say in a boastful manner. “We’re going to stay below the government’s radar.”

Trevor lived a life of seclusion. He had TV, some video game consoles (all pirated to work without internet connection), exercise equipment, board games designed for just two people to play, and a private library of books. He could only enjoy the outdoors when under the watchful eyes of his father. Even then, they never strayed too far from home. Although Dylan Snyder still had some kind of government job that caused him to leave the house four days out of the week, he gave his son stern warnings to prevent any contact with strangers while he was away. Trevor wanted to escape for a bit and glimpse more of the world through his own eyes rather than a screen. Unfortunately, he wasn't allowed to leave sight of home. He knew the argument his dad would make. They had already repeated the conversation a hundred times.

"You're an 'Unregistered Asset,' according to the laws of this land." His father had stated. "If they find out about you, the powers-that-be will take you away. You'll be a slave of their will and comfort, as long as you remain useful."

At which, Trevor would respond, "But, sometimes I feel like a prisoner in my own house, dad. I don't get to meet anyone my age. I'm not allowed to go out and do fun activities other than the same games you and I share, over and over. What fear drives you to keep me here as if I'm a shameful secret?"

Dylan might soften at some of Trevor's excuses, but he proved he would never bend on the issue. "Those shortcomings are still better than being dead. It's not out of shame, but safety that you need to hide here. The government registers everyone's abilities. They assign us jobs without our consent if they desire our talent. Do you want this to happen to you?"

At that point, the father would roll up his sweatpants. He always wore sweatpants; jeans didn't fit well around his one knee, and shorts revealed the ugly deformity on his leg. Dylan never talked about the *why* or *how* of the incident, but somehow, someone's hand had become fused with his knee. Some of the fingers poking out from the skin had been amputated; likewise, the wrist stump protruding out the opposite side had been severed. They never removed the thumb, which happened to run along the one side of his knee, barely protruding above the skin.

"I've seen worse than this on friends of mine who were drafted into the same war. A war we didn't support, but we had no option except to go. We got there, and then the rest became survival." His father would then continue to say, while limping closer. "Some of the powers in existence are very frightening. When you look at this injury, and think about your ability, isn't it possible this could happen to you?"

His father always laid down a convincing argument. Yet, even Trevor wondered how long the threat of unknown dangers would outweigh the growing boredom and wanderlust in his life.

Today, like so many other days, Trevor sat and flipped through TV stations. He watched events in the world around him…a world in which he couldn't take part.

"Another earthquake struck southern Kranston last night. This third incident in as many years has left an estimated 30,000 houses without power, and authorities are still estimating the death toll..."

Click.

"Welcome back to the start of the second round of 'Shows What I Know.' As we move into the next round of trivia categories, we thank the lovely Debbie, our Nullifier, for ensuring the fairness of our competition."

Click.

"... tomorrow night's episode of 'Single and 30,' the bachelor finds out that two of his dating hopefuls have been using psychic suggestions to reduce the playing field..."

Click.

"...so once again, I urge the Senate to reconsider this bill. For too long, genetic seeding without adequate knowledge of results has led to many who suffer as I have. While some people grow up enjoying gifts of flight, abnormal strength, and telekinesis...others are burdened with scaly skin, crippled limbs, and even the inability to breathe outside of water. Every year, we see increased cases of acromegaly, diabetes, Porrick's wasting, heart problems, and organ malformations. Those of us referred to as Afflicted have a large unemployment percentage. We are the majority in homeless statistics..."

"That's all the good our government has done for us." Dylan spoke from behind Trevor, causing the boy to jump. The teen hadn't heard his father enter the room. The middle-aged man pointed at the screen while holding a beer in his hand. "Back in my grandpa's day, they had a revolt to change things. It started out as the common folk against the political elites. The people wanted a government that put the common man's needs first. Everything they pushed was for the good of the whole. Individual freedoms were stamped out in the name of public safety."

The father shook his head. “From what I hear, we haven't made anything easier. I believe some of the same families remain at the top of the political ladder. Any new law that can be twisted ‘for the good of the people’ can be rammed through Congress easily. Even some of the laws that were enacted back in those early revolution days have been twisted from their original intent.”

“Dad, I can't hide here until I'm an old man. What happens when they find out about me?”

“That will be my problem to worry about. I may get prosecuted or jailed, but anything that keeps you safe is worth it. Plus, after you reach a certain age they won't be able to assign you certain jobs anymore. You'll be past the dangerous part. I dread thinking how they might misuse your ability.”

Trevor didn’t know how to express his feelings in a way that wouldn’t invite another lecture from his dad. More than anyone else, Trevor’s talent could take him just about anywhere he desired. There seemed to be no limit to the heights he could attain, or the places he could be. His father’s constant warnings throughout his childhood made him afraid of his own power. It would only take one government sensor to catch a signature from his ability, then they would come for him.

The teen realized he was still staring at a government testimony. As long as the channel remained, his father would undoubtedly keep rambling on about politics. Trevor flipped through a few stations quickly, settling on a nature special. A narrator droned on about changing migratory patterns of North Tanzen waterfowl. The subject bored his father into drinking elsewhere. Ten minutes of feigning interest almost put him to sleep.

His father called from the front door. “Trevor! I’m running to the store to grab some more beer, maybe find a good movie to rent. It will take me a couple hours to get back. You behave yourself.”

Once Trevor heard the wheels pull away, he started daydreaming about where he would go, if he ever was to go somewhere. His thoughts played upon earlier temptations. Like many teens born with a powerful and alluring ability, he wanted to explore its full potential. He discounted the strength of his father's worries. How could the government keep his ability on a leash? How could they stop him from slipping out of their grip? Did they even have the means to track a power like his?

He told himself that he could just use his power sparingly; just as an occasional treat for himself. He planned to do it at times when his father wasn't around, but those moments came seldom at best.

The more he thought about it, the more he realized that this could be the day. He could go somewhere, do something, and no one would know. His nerves tingled in anticipation. But where?

His attention returned to the nature program. One of the camera shots showed a cliff overlooking a lush canyon. Beautiful birds in bright colors soared over the valley. He thought out loud. "That's perfect."

Trevor stood up. He focused on the scene. He fixed the image in his head, closed his eyes, and willed himself there. He felt an immediate change. The air popped as gas was displaced, a humid wind blew across his arms, and strange animal sounds filled his hearing. He reopened his eyes to a dream come true. The teen stood exactly as he had pictured it in his mind.

Except for two details. The first exception took the form of an angry bird. It stood atop a nest that hadn't been present when the show was filmed, and which sat next to his foot. As Trevor backed away from the peeved avian, he also noted the setting sun. His teleport had taken him several time zones eastward.

The young man reflected a bit on this experience. In the course of his life, he'd mostly teleported to places he could see. The only times he'd broken that rule was when he envisioned his room and jumped space to return to it. He hadn't thought much on why he did that until now. Trevor realized he was doing so out of safety before consciously thinking about why. He knew his room was safe and clear in the center. If he'd performed today's trick and aimed a few feet to the side, his body might have merged with the bird's. He recalled the image of the unknown hand merged within his dad's leg. That nightmare took center stage in his mind. Trevor realized the dangers of teleporting blindly, without knowing any changes at the destination. The program he watched on TV might have been filmed years ago, prior to the bird making his home here. In addition, the sun was setting. He might have blindly teleported into a rainstorm, tornado, forest fire, or other climate hazard.

The deeper fear soon receded, especially in light of the pleasant assault on his senses. He could see strange trees and colorful birds, smell new flower scents riding the air, feel the air currents teasing his hair. A part of him felt almost giddy with freedom. He stood maybe a quarter of the world away from his house! He shouted the thought inside his mind, alongside personal gratitudes of his daring journey. As a Teleporter, he had always known that the whole world lay within his reach. Unless his father disallowed it, which he did.

"Dad, you'd be so mad at me now." He raised both arms to the sky. "A hundred percent worth it!" Trevor launched forth a howl at the air. Not too different from a wolf howl, it echoed across the canyon and back to his ears.

Within minutes, Trevor opened the door from his bedroom and peeked down the hall. No sign of dad. He had worried that he might get caught. What if the car had broken down and his father hiked back and looked for him? He cautiously checked the house, confirming that his father hadn't returned. Despite all his worries, the joy of freedom allured him. He planned to test fate again. He wanted to find a live TV feed and safely teleport somewhere else. Deciding to get a little more insurance in case his father came back unexpectedly, he went back to his room and set the scene. He covered some pillows with blankets, making it look like he might be napping. Then, Trevor turned on the radio, though he didn't blast the music. He adjusted just enough volume to cover why he might not have heard dad calling for him. He also did a more thorough clean up of the center of his room to ensure against being a little off on his teleport.

Switching TV channels, he paused at one which showed some kind of celebration. He recognized the locale as a city only four hours away. News announcers chatted about some noisy fireworks going off, while a few kids ran through a field in the background. A carnival atmosphere dominated the foreground. It intrigued him…but how would he get there without a commotion? It didn't take him long to find his moment. There was an open spot in the background between two buildings. Cars were slowly moving in front of it, driving slowly past the carnival grounds. He just had to time his jump so that a sizable car blocked the TV's line of sight to the alley. He kneeled down like he was tying his shoe. When his moment came, he fixed the scene in his mind and blinked.

Trevor's teleport went off faster this time. He stood up and wandered into the carnival atmosphere. The youth stood in awe of the scene before him. He saw other teenagers openly displaying some of their powers; some carnival events even catered to it. He saw people using telekinesis to launch sandbags at targets. Some youths used either parkour, flight, or super speed to be the first to conquer an obstacle course. Although, he felt he might gag when he saw a freak show featuring those whose gift only brought them deformities. Society labeled them as Afflicted. Trevor knew about them from TV, but had never seen one in person.

He quickly turned away from the spectacle and moved on to other interests. Despite the fact he brought only a little cash in his pocket, Trevor went on to have the best day of his life. It even culminated in winning a stuffed animal prize for a random girl, who then expressed her admiration by giving him a hug and a quick peck on the cheek. He barely got home in time before his father returned, but he knew he would be doing this again as soon as he could.

***

Ring…ring…

Gordon Rogers rolled over and searched for his phone. His hand slapped around the hotel nightstand until he managed to snag it. Sitting up, he peeked one bleary eye at the time on the clock: 07:35AM. He'd been hoping to sleep past nine.

He forced a calm tone as he answered. "You know I'm on vacation, remember?"

The female voice on the other end replied, "At that chateau in the Tomoan mountains, correct? Tell me that you're still there."

Gordon spoke firmly. "I plan to be here for at least three more days. Call someone else, Jen."

"You're going to cut it short, and I don't think you'll be too disappointed…" Jen started to say.

"What is this?"

"We have a RE emergency, code 206: UT."

Gordon threw a hand up, not that his accomplice could see the motion. "What is so urgent about this Unregistered Talent that you need me."

"He or she is a Teleporter." Jen paused for his reaction.

Gordon went silent and motionless as he considered the implications. His thousand-yard stare went well past the confines of the room. All of the sudden, his training and profession took on a whole new meaning. His voice wavered a bit as he asked. "Did I hear you correctly? A Teleporter?"

"Yes. You're not only the closest one to the location, you've also got the best ability to counteract and bring him in..."

"They're trusting me to do this alone? No backup?" Gordon's hands felt sweaty.

She answered, "HQ already cross-checked the talents of the local police force. They can't stop this kid from teleporting if he decides to run. You can."

"Kid?" Gordon grabbed the hotel's complimentary pen and notepad from the nightstand and began jotting down notes. "What do we know about our subject?"

"Scanners have been picking up displacement waves over the last few months. We began to triangulate an origin spot in those mountains, but didn't get a better fix until we installed some new scanners."

Gordon considered the information. "Someone hid a kid away in these mountains? That may have been going on for years. That's why he's unregistered?"

Jen replied, "Yes. When we started doing background checks of the residents up there, we struck a promising lead with a retired Fireshaper, Dylan Snyder. He's a veteran of two campaigns: Ganung Border War, and Krisanth's Rebellion. Around seventeen years ago, he and his wife went through the rounds of genetic seeding in preparation for a pregnancy. They disappeared for ten months until he reported her death in an accidental fire."

Gordon's head rose up, "A Fireshaper's wife died in a fire?"

Jen added, "Or died in some other way, such as childbirth, and the burn wounds concealed evidence of the pregnancy. Dylan didn't part with the military on good terms. He may have had a reason for hiding a child."

Gordon considered the situation. "I'm glad you gave me the chance to take care of this."

She replied. "You only get one chance. HQ is also mobilizing a specialized strike team to take him in if you fail."

"I don't think that's going to help the overall goal here." Gordon sighed. "I'm on the case."

***

Gordon eased his rental car up to the cabin. He didn't expect any warm welcome…except that which a Fireshaper could throw at him. The Nullifier ability could stop Dylan Snyder from attacking him directly, but he could still be humanly vulnerable to a normal fire once started. He'd already had to cut the chain lock on the "private property" fence. He wasn't sure whether to believe the "Beware of Dog" sign, but he was glad he had carried his sidearm on vacation. Even in a world of magical abilities, Gordon's talent offered only defense. He'd been forced to use his gun in the past.

He hoped it wouldn't come down to that. A teleporter, especially a teen, could decide to jump half a world away in the blink of an eye if panicked. Gordon needed time to talk to the kid.

As he parked the car near the door and stepped out, Gordon's talent reached out with maximum effort to deflect any ambush. He held out his badge and walked up to the door. He glanced in all directions. He saw a barn, ditch, junk heap, two cars (one rusted from years of neglect), and a tool shed. No sign of any dog, but plenty of ambush spots nearby. He rapped his knuckles on the door with all the authority of his office. He believed he could hear two sets of voices in the house. One told the other to stay out of sight.

The door opened, revealing a worn-looking, middle-aged man. Gordon recognized Dylan from the service pics Jen had sent him, although many years had transpired. The look Dylan gave him wasn't friendly, to say the least.

"Mister," Dylan barked, "you need to vacate my property now. My ability can kill."

Gordon flashed his badge. "I need to have a talk with you and your child. It's impor…"

Gordon didn't get a chance to finish. As soon as the homeowner realized that the government had come for his son, he tried to kill the agent. Dylan extended a hand and willed fire to the tip of his fingers. Gordon saw the man's surprised look when he realized that was as far as his talent could extend. The attempt made the agent's skin tingle.

The homeowner jumped backwards, getting his hands on the door to slam it. Gordon expected the move and was quick to get his body through the opening.

"We need to talk!" Gordon shouted.

Dylan refused to cooperate. He reached for a thick walking cane located just inside the door. Both men got their hands on it, trying to get the advantage of the other. They shoved and spun around in the front hallway.

Gordon saw a teenage boy's head peek out from further down the hall. He wasn't sure how he might get a chance to speak peacefully with how defensive the father acted. If the government agent was under a deadlier threat, he had his sidearm…but then the teleporter would be gone and it would be much harder to get any cooperation. Somehow, Gordon Rogers had to get both son and father to cooperate…despite the violent start.

For all the ferociousness at which the disabled former veteran tried to defend his home and child, the government agent possessed muscles and skills from years of gym training and martial arts. Such exercises were the only thing that could give him an advantage. Gordon Rogers leveraged the cane into a favorable position. Dylan let out a fierce yell, foreseeing the outcome but unable to alter it. The RE Operative smashed the cane into the side of the father's head. Gordon swept the legs from under the homeowner, hearing and feeling him smack heavily against the floor. Dylan stopped moving, though they could hear him breath.

"Dad!"

The boy came running out of the back hall. His eyes flicked between his father and the agent on top of him. Gordon felt like he could sense the boy's thoughts. He wanted to rescue his dad by teleportation, but he didn't want to get close to a man he considered a threat. The teen hesitated a few steps away.

Gordon took command of the situation. "Get me an ice pack to help your father. Look for a first aid kit, too." The kid didn't listen. He ran forward, grabbed his dad, and closed his eyes. The agent's skin tingled as he counteracted the teleport. The kid's eyes opened in surprise. "That won't work. Quickly, ice and gauze. We need to assist your father."

Gordon could feel some blood under the man's head. It wouldn't be a serious injury once they could get him to the hospital, but he needed to secure the boy's trust and time.

***

Gordon and Trevor sat down across from each other in a private room inside the hospital. They'd only spoken a few words while transporting his dad to the ER. The agent began, "Trevor, I want you to know first and foremost, that neither you nor your dad did anything wrong that can't be forgiven if you can help us out."

"I'm unregistered. You're going to try to take me away, aren't you? What's to stop me from going home?"

"Nothing," Gordon admitted. When he saw the doubt in Trevor's eyes, he explained. "I'm not here to persecute you because you are unregistered. You and your father broke the law, but there is a bigger issue involved. Also, if you decide to run, there is little the government can do to stop you, but it *will* try, and you won't like their methods."

Trevor's face hardened. Gordon raised a calming hand. "But listen to me first. We need you. Teleportation is the rarest talent of all, and it's the one key ability that is missing from Project Ark."

"What is Project Ark?"

Gordon glanced around the empty room, but since he was broadcasting his nullifier ability, no one should be peeping in on their conversation. "Project Ark is a government plan to save the people of this planet. Have you heard about all those earthquakes in the last few years?" The boy nodded. Gordon continued. "What the public doesn't know is that in the next twenty to thirty years, there'll be a supervolcanic eruption near the north polar cap. The expected magnitude will be enough to wipe out most life on this planet."

He allowed the teen to digest the news. After a minute, Trevor asked, "All of these mutated powers, and no one can fix it?"

Gordon nodded. "I'm afraid so. Lots of hypotheses have been thrown out, a few tests run. Unfortunately, we've made matters worse. The timeline has encroached forward."

"Why do you need a Teleporter?"

The agent looked the teen straight in the eyes. "Because it's time to go interstellar. Ark has been mapping out distant worlds and assembling the core talents we need to make terraforming possible on another planet. I'm told that the one ability they lacked to make the whole thing possible, is a Teleporter. We can't fix our own planet; but with some combined powers, we can tame a new one. According to all the data and simulations they've run, it would be easier to terraform than alter our own planet anymore. Plus, it opens up settlement across the galaxy."

Trevor looked past a wall. "I know how dad is going to react."

Gordon pointed at the youth. "You're our last hope. You are now the star player in a brand new ball game. I think you'll be able to negotiate some perks."

***

Six years later.

Lieutenant Trevor Snyder enjoyed the view outside the forward screen. His fourth visit to space, and it was finally time to take the biggest leap in human history. He took a glance at his fellow teammates on the ship's bridge. These were the finest talents the world could find to start a new home elsewhere.

A Telekinetic piloted the ship. He could control the entire vessel with his thoughts and hold it together under high stress.

Lt. Angelica Statham, the girl to his left, was called a Farseer. She had to sit with her head locked into a device which would help her stay steady as she viewed a planet light years away. The amazing thing about her ability: she could view its exact position in real-time, undistorted by light's speed.

Two people sat in such a way that they could touch both Trevor and Angelica at the same time, meaning one sat facing to the rear. The first one, an Amplifier named Lt. Vance Vang, already had his hand on her shoulder. His Amplifier talent boosted other people's abilities, which allowed her to see far away into space with such perfect clarity. The second person, facing to the rear, had one hand on Trevor's knee, the other on Angelica's. He would help Trevor see through her eyes in order to teleport there.

Angelica said, "Ok Mindlink, I have it."

In the lower decks sat several more crew members. A Windmixer and a Plantsinger would be instrumental in transforming the air and flora of the new world into a life-giving biosphere. A Geomancer came along for testing and altering the soil. A Weathervane would help tame harsh conditions on the new world. A Planefolder could anchor two points and create a dimensional bridge, which would link a permanent "door" from one planet to the other. At least four other crew members would help sustain the crew with summoned goods or medical assistance.

The Mindlink connected Trevor to Angelica. A moment later, Trevor felt the touch on his shoulder from their Amplifier, Vance. Vance's skill would also boost his, allowing Trevor to teleport the entire ship at once.

Trevor saw the new planet. It was blue and green, swirling with clouds, and bathed in the light of its sun. A brave new world awaited.

His only sorrowful thought centered around the man that gave him this path. Gordon Rogers never mentioned it, but Nullifiers like him would never benefit from this solution. They couldn't be teleported, nor walk through dimensional bridges. They would be stranded on a dying, deserted planet.

But, at least for billions of others, there would be a future of hope under distant suns. As everyone signaled the green light, Trevor Snyder took them all on a leap farther than anyone had once dreamed possible.

The End

About the Author

Born in 1971, Douglas Van Dyke Jr is an award-winning author that mostly writes fantasy tales in the realm called Dhea Loral. It is a world in which readers are rewarded by characters and events making appearances across different book series. Many of his characters evolved in RPG and MMORPG games, further developing their own personalities.

His epic trilogy intro, "The Earthrin Stones," sold a surprising amount and received some blushing praise. Both "The Widow Brigade" and "Apprentice Storm Mage" won BRAG honors in 2023. He's also been begged to submit stories for at least two to three anthologies a year, which so far he's been fulfilling.

He's taught schoolchildren about writing, tours several Midwest conventions during the year, sends out at least one newsletter/month, and works in medical imaging.

Other books by this author

Please visit your favorite retailer to discover other books by Douglas Van Dyke Jr:
(As of Fall, 2025)

The Earthrin Stones Trilogy
Inheritance of a Sword and a Path
Trials of Faith
Muster of Heroes

The Pilgrims with Blades Series
A01 - Pressed into Service
A02 - Grandfather's Castle
A03 - Caravan Road

Storm-Mage Chronicles
Apprentice Storm Mage
Daughter of the Legend

Other Titles based in the Fantasy World of Dhea Loral
The Widow Brigade
The Wooden Maiden

Other Worlds
Boxer Earns His Wings
Misadventures of RPG Dice
The Pale Gunner (Chapter 2 of "The Time of Champions" by Christopher D Schmitz)

Anthologies
Otherworldly: A Genre Fiction Anthology, Volumes 1, 2, & 3
Streets of Fire and Shadow

Laser Cannons and First Contact
Wonders and Dragons: A Midwest Fantasy Sampler: 2025

Connect with Douglas Van Dyke Jr

I really appreciate you reading my free story! Here are my social media outlets:

Visit my website, learn how to contact me directly, and/or sign up for my mailing list: https://dhealoral.com
Follow me on Facebook: https://www.facebook.com/DheaLoral
Follow me on Twitter: https://twitter.com/ThaminDheaLoral

Give my books a review and some stars at your favorite retailer! That is the equivalent of clapping your hands at the end of the show, and letting me know you want more. Indie-authors depend on word-of-mouth to generate publicity.

Want to experience the world of Dhea Loral? Explore the dwarf homelands through the eyes of revolutionary Duli! *The Widow Brigade* opened on Amazon with numerous praises and won a BRAG medallion in 2023! This story features strong women, in a fantasy setting, rebelling against the traditions of a male-dominated society.

"I felt the plot was well developed, well-paced, and the motivations of the characters really drew me in, caring about what happened as the plot progressed. I felt the main character was not your typical shiny hero, or dastardly anti-hero. She just felt real. I highly recommend this book..." - Tom H

"This book is very well written and as always with his stories, the battle scenes are intense, with details that pull you in and fully immerse yourself in the story. The characters are well developed and allow you to enjoy loving and hating them." – Lockhart

The *Earthrin Stones* trilogy introduced readers to Dhea Loral, offering the largest backstory and plot driving the scenes of this world. Open your adventure with *Inheritance of a Sword and a Path*!

"Over a thousand years ago the Godswars ravaged the land of Dhea Loral, shattering continents, laying waste to cities, and driving species to extinction. The people of the land are once again starting to prosper and flourish, while the gods stay aloft and watch from afar the recovery. Yet, not all the old quarrels have been forgotten. For some gods, the time is right to once again meddle in the affairs of mortals. Though the gods have bound themselves by a Covenant that bars their direct entry into Dhea Loral, they are able to send mortal emissaries to carry out their schemes."

"*Inheritance of a Sword and a Path* is a treasure trove of fantasy, eye-popping adventures, lead characters imbued with morality, humility, strength and humor…This saga opener had me turning pages, reading way (way) past my bedtime, and definitely curious for the next installment. Pure fun!" — Lori Crever, host. "30 Minutes with the Author"

Check out the author's other BRAG award-winning YA fantasy: *Apprentice Storm Mage.*

Fire and Ashes! The city is burning!

Young mage's apprentice Thomena is gifted in the elements of wind and water, but she yearns to learn the secrets of fire. When she discovers another mage is the one starting fires around her city of Orlaun, her resolve is tested by tragedy and roaring infernos. She needs to win the trust of the toughest heroes around, the fire-fighting vigiles, but they are hard to impress. Can she save Orlaun before the fires consume all Thomena cares about?

Pick up this coming-of-age adventure which opens up a new chapter in the fantasy realm of Dhea Loral.

"What made the story so exciting for me was the main character; she is a young woman who is always working to better herself. She's not about power or fame, but simply internal improvement. This leads to her facing the challenges of the book with a surprisingly humble competence ... I look forward to reading more stories of her in future books." —Michael Bernabo, Author of The Renaissance Army series.

Strangers thrown together, forced into service on a common quest, form a bond of camaraderie. Each seeks to find their focus in the world, amidst their private mysteries.

The half-orc savage, who takes pride in a company he no longer serves. The dusk-skinned archer, carrying a bow from her forgotten homeland. The dwarf who studies the past so he can create a future. The knight who pays fealty to no lord. The elf sorceress seeking knowledge, but what specific question is she trying to answer?

They will band together, seeking separate goals. How far will pilgrims travel to discover who they are?

-Pilgrims with Blades: Pressed into Service-

Facing a crisis and looking for any excuse to strike in force against the orcs occupying the hills to their south, the city-state Kashmer conscripts privateers and adventurers into war. A band of strangers must learn to support and adapt to each other as a daring plan separates them from the main force in hostile territory. Each possess their own mystery, but without cooperation and trust, they will be doomed to failure.

Pressed into Service is the introduction to the bold Pilgrims with Blades series.

Dhea Loral

www.ingramcontent.com/pod-product-compliance
Lightning Source LLC
LaVergne TN
LVHW010921110826
845155LV00038B/712

* 9 7 8 1 9 4 9 0 6 0 1 6 4 *